For Joel G. —K.B.

For my parents, who adopted a dog for me and changed my life. —N.S.

Text copyright © 2017 by Kate Banks

Jacket art and interior illustrations copyright © 2017 by Naoko Stoop

All rights reserved. Published in the United States by Schwartz & Wade Books,

an imprint of Random House Children's Books, a division of Penguin Random House LLC, New York.

Schwartz & Wade Books and the colophon are trademarks of Penguin Random House LLC.

Visit us on the Web! randomhousekids.com

Educators and librarians, for a variety of teaching tools, visit us at RHTeachersLibrarians.com

*Library of Congress Cataloging-in-Publication Data*

Names: Banks, Kate, author. | Stoop, Naoko, illustrator.

Title: Pup and bear / Kate Banks ; illustrated by Naoko Stoop.

Description: First Edition. | New York : Schwartz & Wade Books, 2017. | Summary: A stranded wolf cub is rescued and raised by a loving polar bear,

and years later when he is grown into a wolf and on his own, he comes upon a lost polar bear cub, and the cycle begins again.

Identifiers: LCCN 2016047526 | ISBN 978-0-399-55409-4 (hardback) | ISBN 978-0-399-55410-0 (glb) | ISBN 978-0-399-55411-7 (ebook)

Subjects: | CYAC: Mothers and child—Fiction. | Parental behavior in animals—Fiction. | Wolves—Fiction. | Polar bear—Fiction. | Bears—Fiction. |

Arctic regions—Fiction. | BISAC: JUVENILE FICTION / Family / Alternative Family. | JUVENILE FICTION / People & Places / Polar Regions.

Classification: LCC PZ7.B22594 Pu 2017 | DDC [E]—dc23

The text of this book is set in Bembo.

The illustrations were rendered in acrylic paint, ink, pencils, and pastels on plywood, and digitally finished.

MANUFACTURED IN CHINA

2 4 6 8 10 9 7 5 3 1

First Edition

# Pup and Bear

By Kate Banks

Illustrated by Naoko Stoop

schwartz & wade books · new york

# WHOOSH!

When the great gray owl swooped down,
screeching *whoo-whoo,*
the Arctic wolves knew that the Big Freeze
was on its way.

They took shelter in a snowdrift,
and they listened to the fierce wind holler and roar.
They watched the snow blow in spirals,
wrapping the world in a fluffy white coat.

But then the wind's bitter-cold breath turned warm
and the sun appeared.
The Big Melt came,
and one lone pup found itself on a sheet of ice
spinning out to sea.

The pup slid into the water. He swam and he swam.
When he reached land, he burrowed into a snowbank.
He was tired and he wanted his mother.

The pup closed his eyes and fell asleep,
listening to the throb of silence
across the still landscape.

He woke to the feel of a cold nose against his fur.
The smell was familiar. It was a polar bear.

"You are not my mother," said the pup,
flattening his ears against his head.
"I am not your mother," said the polar bear,
"but I can cuddle you and keep you safe."

The pup was shy and frightened.
"Aren't you going to eat me?" he asked.
"Polar bears eat wolves."

"Not this one," said the polar bear, shaking her head.
"Climb on my back, and I will take you to my den."

The pup stretched a paw forward cautiously.
Then he climbed onto the polar bear's back,

and they crossed the tundra under the watchful eyes
of a trio of baby puffins learning to fly.

Back at the den, the polar bear licked and cleaned the pup.
"I am not your mother," she said,
"but I can feed you and keep you warm."

The next day they set off across the wintry tundra.

When they spotted a walrus with long, sharp tusks,
the polar bear bellowed and chuffed.

"Where are we going?" asked the pup
as they neared the water.
"I am not your mother," said the polar bear,
"but I can show you where to catch a fish."

They passed a snow goose
perched on a nest of eggs.

They sniffed the trail of a seal
as he tried to outsmart them.

And they stopped at the water's edge,
where the fish and the lemmings
came and went
in the wondrous wheel of life.

The sun shone down on the crisp, crackling snow,
and the polar bear rolled in a snowbank.
"Come on," she said to the pup.
"I am not your mother,
but I can play with you."

But when the pup tugged too hard at the polar bear's fur,
the bear growled.
"I am not your mother," she said,
"but I can scold you."
Then she nuzzled the pup and tickled his tummy.

Tired at last, the pup curled up against the bear,
and they napped, listening to the wind whimper and sigh.

The Earth turned round and round.
And the Big Freeze came, followed by the Big Melt,
until at last the polar bear nudged the wolf,
who wasn't a pup any longer.
"I am not your mother," she said,
"but I know it's time for you to go."
She nuzzled the wolf one last time,
and the wolf nuzzled her back.

Then he walked out into the wide world.

The wolf howled to the midnight sun,
which glowed on the horizon,
where day ended and night began.
And he was answered by the cry of another wolf.

Soon he was leading his own pack across the frozen tundra.

Then one day the wolf came upon
a polar bear cub huddled in a snowdrift.
"Where is your mother?" asked the wolf.
But the cub didn't know.

The wolf sniffed the cub and rubbed
its fur with a wet nose.
"You are not my mother," said the cub, cowering.
"I am not your mother," said the wolf,
"but I can cuddle you and keep you warm."

"Aren't you going to eat me?" asked the cub.

"Wolves eat polar bears."

"Not this one," said the wolf, shaking its head.

"Climb on my back and I will take you to my den."

The polar bear clambered onto the wolf's back.
"I am not your mother," said the wolf,
"but you can stay with me until you're big enough
to be on your own."

And the wolf led the pack back across the tundra,
along the path that went round and round
in the wondrous wheel of life.